This Little Tiger book belongs to:

_____

_____

_____

For Anna
– SS

To Mum, Dad and his
delicious vegetable soup
– JD

LITTLE TIGER PRESS LTD,
an imprint of the Little Tiger Group
1 The Coda Centre, 189 Munster Road, London SW6 6AW
www.littletiger.co.uk

First published in Great Britain 2006
This edition published 2016

Text copyright © Steve Smallman 2006
Illustrations copyright © Joëlle Dreidemy 2006
Steve Smallman and Joëlle Dreidemy have asserted their
rights to be identified as the author and illustrator of this
work under the Copyright, Designs and Patents Act, 1988

A CIP catalogue record for this book is available
from the British Library

Printed in China • LTP/1400/1887/0417

10 9 8 7 6 5 4 3 2

THE LAMB WHO CAME FOR DINNER

STEVE SMALLMAN   JOËLLE DREIDEMY

LITTLE TIGER
LONDON

"Vegetable soup AGAIN!" moaned the old wolf. "Oh, I wish I had a little lamb. I could make a hotpot, my favourite!"
    Just then . . .

KNOCK!
KNOCK!

It was a little lamb. "Can I come in?" the little lamb said. "Yes, my dear, do come in. You're just in time for dinner!" sniggered the old wolf.

The little lamb was
shivering with cold.
BRRRR! BRRRR! she went.
 "GOODNESS GRACIOUS ME!"
said the old wolf. "I can't eat
a lamb that's frozen. I HATE
frozen food!"
 So he put her next to the
fire to thaw her out.

The old wolf looked up
a recipe for lamb hotpot.
Mmmmmm! He felt hungry
just at the thought of it.

The lamb was feeling hungry too. Her tummy rumbled. RUMBLE! RUMBLE! RUMBLE! it went. "GOODNESS GRACIOUS ME!" said the old wolf. "I can't eat a lamb with a rumbling tummy. I might get indigestion!"

So he gave the lamb a carrot to eat. "Stuffing," he said to himself.

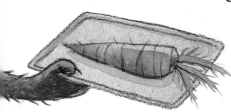

The little lamb gobbled
down the carrot so quickly
that she got hiccups!

HIC,
HIC,
HICCUP!

she went.

"GOODNESS GRACIOUS ME!"
said the old wolf. "I can't
eat a lamb with hiccups!
I might catch them too!"
But he didn't know how
to cure hiccups.

He tried throwing the lamb up in the air.

HIC!

That didn't work.

He held her upside-down.

HIC!

That didn't work.

So the old wolf put the lamb over
his shoulder and patted her back with
his big hairy paw.
  The lamb stopped hiccupping, snuggled
under the old wolf's shaggy chin and fell
fast asleep in his arms. The old wolf felt
funny. He'd never been hugged by his
dinner before and suddenly he didn't feel
so hungry after all.

The little lamb snored gently in his ear.
SNORE! SNORE! she went.
  "Goodness gracious me!" whispered the
old wolf. "I can't eat a lamb that's snoring!"

The old wolf sat down in the chair by the fire, the little lamb warm on his chest, and thought just how very long it had been since anyone had given him a cuddle.

He sniffed, then sniffed again. The little lamb smelt so . . . so . . . DELICIOUS! "Oh!" groaned the wolf. "If I eat her quickly, it'll be all right." And he was just about to gobble her up when . . .

... she woke up and gave him a great big kiss.

SMACK!

"NOOO!!!"

howled the wolf, "THAT'S NOT FAIR! I am a big, bad WOLF and you are ... hotpot!" "Hop-pop!" said the little lamb with a smile. Then she pointed at the old wolf and said, "Woof!" "Oh, give me strength!" groaned the old wolf. "You'll have to go!"

He wrapped the little lamb up warmly and put her outside.

"NOW GO AWAY!"

he shouted. "If you stay here, I'll eat you, and then we'll both be sorry!" And he shut the door with a

BANG!

It was dark outside, and cold.
The little lamb banged on the door.
"Woof?" she cried. "Can I come in, Woof?"
But the old wolf stuck his fingers in his ears
and went "LA! LA! LA!" until she stopped.
At last, all was quiet. "Thank goodness she's gone!"
thought the wolf. "She's not safe here with
a hungry old wolf like me."

Then he thought of the lamb,
all alone in the dark wood.

"She might get lost!"

"She might get frozen!"

"She might get eaten!"

"OH NO,
WHAT HAVE I DONE?"

he howled. He leapt up and
opened the door.
The lamb was gone.

The old wolf rushed out into the
dark wood, crying, "Little lamb!
Little lamb! Come back!
I won't eat you . . . I promise!"

Much, much later, a sad, soggy old wolf trudged wearily back to his cottage alone.

He pushed open the door and there, by the fire,
sat the little lamb!

"YOU CAME BACK!" said the wolf with
a smile. "Haven't you got anywhere else to go?"

The little lamb shook her head.

"Er . . . er . . . then would you like to
stay here . . . with me?" asked the wolf.

The little lamb gave him a hard stare.
"Not eat me, Woof, no?" she said.

"GOODNESS GRACIOUS ME!" said
the old wolf. "I can't eat a lamb
who needs me! I might
get heartburn!"

The little lamb
smiled and then
threw herself into
the old wolf's
arms.

"Are you feeling
hungry, Hotpot?"
asked the wolf.

"How about some vegetable soup?
It's my favourite."

More fabulous books from Little Tiger Press!

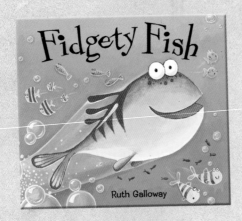

Fidgety Fish

Ruth Galloway

Gillian Lobel

Little Honey Bear and the Smiley Moon

Tim Warnes

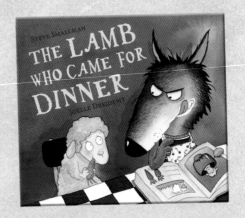

STEVE SMALLMAN

THE LAMB WHO CAME FOR DINNER

JOËLLE DREIDEMY

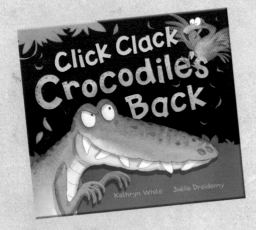

Click Clack Crocodile's Back

Kathryn White   Joëlle Dreidemy

Puppy's First Christmas

Steve Smallman
Alison Edgson

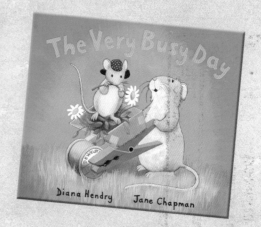

The Very Busy Day

Diana Hendry   Jane Chapman

For information regarding any of the above titles
or for our catalogue, please contact us:
Little Tiger Press, 1 The Coda Centre,
189 Munster Road, London SW6 6AW
Tel: 020 7385 6333
E-mail: contact@littletiger.co.uk
www.littletiger.co.uk